# MUSEUM
# MYSTERIES

Museum Mysteries is published by Stone Arch Books
A Capstone Imprint
1710 Roe Crest Drive
North Mankato, Minnesota 56003
www.mycapstone.com

Text and illustrations © 2019 Stone Arch Books

Library of Congress Cataloging-in-Publication Data

Names: Brezenoff, Steven, author. | Weber, Lisa K., illustrator. |
    Brezenoff, Steven. Museum mysteries.
Title: The case of the new professor / by Steve Brezenoff ; illustrated
by Lisa K. Weber.
Description: North Mankato, Minnesota : Stone Arch Books, a Capstone
    imprint, [2019] | Series: Museum mysteries | Summary: Someone is
    messing with the Museum of Natural History, mixing human models from
    the new Pleistocene Megafauna in with the dinosaur exhibits, and
    Wilson Kipper, whose mother works in the museum as a paleontologist,
    and his friends are determined to find out who is responsible for
    the anti-science vandalism—the new professor, her nasty daughter,
    or someone else entirely.
Identifiers: LCCN 2018044107| ISBN 9781496578181 (hardcover) |
    ISBN 9781496580238 (pbk.) | ISBN 9781496578204 (ebook pdf)
Subjects: LCSH: Natural history museums—Juvenile fiction. | Vandalism—
    Juvenile fiction. | Pseudoscience—Juvenile fiction. | Detective and
    mystery stories. | CYAC: Mystery and detective stories. | Natural
    history museums—Fiction. | Museums—Fiction. | Vandalism—Fiction. |
    Science--Fiction. | GSAFD: Mystery fiction. | LCGFT: Detective and
    mystery fiction.
Classification: LCC PZ7.B7576 Can 2019 | DDC 813.6 [Fic]—dc23
LC record available at https://lccn.loc.gov/2018044107

Design Elements by Shutterstock

Printed and bound in the USA.
PA49

# The Case of the
# NEW PROFESSOR

By Steve Brezenoff
Illustrated by Lisa K. Weber

STONE ARCH BOOKS
a capstone imprint

# Early Hominids

- HOMINIDS WERE ANIMAL-LIKE HUMANS WHO WALKED UPRIGHT. IT IS BELIEVED THE EARLIEST HOMINIDS LIVED AS MANY AS 6–7 MILLION YEARS AGO IN THE FORESTS OF EASTERN AND SOUTHERN AFRICA.

- THESE HOMINIDS ARE BELIEVED TO HAVE BEEN 3–6 FEET TALL AND LIKELY LIVED ON A DIET OF ON LEAVES, FRUITS, AND THE REMAINS OF DEAD ANIMALS.

- SCIENTISTS DIVIDE HOMINIDS INTO DIFFERENT CATEGORIES, INCLUDING HOMO HABILIS, HOMO ERECTUS, AND HOMO SAPIENS. THESE GROUPS ARE BASED ON BODY SHAPES AND LIFESTYLES.

- HOMO HABLIS TRANSLATES TO, "A PERSON WITH ABILITIES." THESE HOMINIDS LIKELY LIVED 1.5 MILLION YEARS AGO.

- HOMO ERECTUS MEANS, "A PERSON WHO WALKS UPRIGHT." THESE HOMINIDS LIVED ON EARTH UNTIL ROUGHLY 150,000 YEARS AGO.

- HOMO SAPIENS MEANS, "A PERSON WHO CAN THINK." ALL HUMAN BEINGS ALIVE TODAY ARE HOMO SAPIENS.

Amal Farah

Raining Sam

Wilson Kipper

Clementine Wim

# Capitol City Sleuths

### Amal Farah
Age: 11
Favorite Museum: Air and Space Museum
Interests: astronomy, space travel, and
building models of spaceships

### Raining Sam
Age: 12
Favorite Museum: American History Museum
Interests: Ojibwe history, culture, and
traditions, American history—good and bad

### Clementine Wim
Age: 13
Favorite Museum: Art Museum
Interests: painting, sculpting with clay, and
anything colorful

### Wilson Kipper
Age: 10
Favorite Museum: Natural History Museum
Interests: dinosaurs (especially pterosaurs
and herbivores) and building dinosaur models

# TABLE OF
# CONTENTS

## CHAPTER 1
## School's Out

"Spring break," Wilson Kipper said. He stood on a flat boulder in the middle of the Big Lawn, located in the center of Museum Campus, and looked up at the pale blue sky.

Lying nearby, Clementine Wim smiled up at him from her spot on the ground. She was one of his best friends, despite the fact that she was four years older than him and more than a foot taller.

"A whole week of no school," she said. "This is my kind of Monday morning." She pointed up at the sky. "That one looks like a giraffe."

"I can see that," Wilson replied.

It was obvious which cloud she meant, although some people might not have noticed. Clem was an artist, and she saw art in everything. Wilson had gotten used to seeing the world that way too.

"Hey, you two!" a familiar voice called.

Wilson turned and shielded his eyes from the sun. It was Amal Farah, one of their other best friends. She was followed by Raining Sam, the last friend to round out their foursome.

The kids were a natural group. Each had a parent who worked at one of Capitol City's major museums: Air and Space, Natural History, Art, and American History. Today, the first day of their spring break, they'd all agreed to meet on the Big Lawn that touched the back of each museum. The lawn rose on a gentle slope to the highest point in the center, where a flat rock marked the spot.

Amal and Raining joined Wilson on the rock.

"Spring," Clementine said.

Her three friends looked down at her.

Clementine looked past her friends, up at the sky, and added, "The vernal equinox."

"Is in three weeks," Wilson corrected her. "It's still winter, technically speaking."

"Yeah, yeah," Clem said, waving him off as she sat up. "It feels like spring. And we're off from school, so that's good enough for me."

"What are we going to do today?" Amal asked. She hopped off the rock and gave Clem's sneakered foot a little kick.

"Let's go inside the Natural History Museum," Wilson said. His mom was a paleontologist at the museum, and it was his favorite place. "My mom's new exhibit is opening."

"What is it?" Raining asked.

"Well, it's not dinosaurs," Wilson said, "but it is prehistoric animals—the giant mammals of the Ice Age. I'm pretty interested."

"Aw, let's stay out here," Clementine said. She turned her face up to the sun again and closed her eyes. "The rebirth of the planet, of all the green things, of long and sunny days, is a moment to celebrate! It has been since the dawn of time!"

"I'm not staying out here to worship the sun," Amal said. "It's not worth the sunburn. Besides, there's nowhere to sit down. Come on, Clem."

"Let's use the back entrance," Wilson said. "There are protestors out front this morning."

"What are they protesting now?" Raining asked.

All the museums got their fair share of protestors from time to time. Some protested a new work of art on loan from a controversial collection. Others protested science they disagreed with at the Air and Space Museum or the Natural History Museum. Still others protested one of the famous Americans noted at the American History Museum.

Wilson shrugged. "I didn't look very closely," he said, "but they were there when Mom and I pulled up this morning."

"I recognized a few of them when we walked past," Amal said.

"They're flat-Earth supporters. They were protesting at air & space last weekend."

"Flat Earth?" Wilson said. "That's ridiculous!"

"Scientifically, yes," Clementine agreed with a shrug. "But you have to admit, there's something sort of appealing about it—imagine the world having an edge you could sit on and dangle your legs off."

Together the four friends walked through the wet grass to the Natural History Museum's rear entrance. The museum wouldn't open to the public for another ninety minutes, but since Wilson's mom worked there, they'd be allowed in. All the guards knew the kids.

"The exhibit doesn't officially open until tomorrow," Wilson said. He led his three best friends around the ropes designed to block the new exhibit from most visitors. "Of course, we get an early peek."

The four friends nearly always got a special early look at new exhibits at all four museums. Another perk of their parents' jobs.

Wilson pointed to a big sign hanging above the doorway to the new exhibit. PLEISTOCENE MEGAFAUNA it read.

"That means 'huge animals of the Ice Age,'" Wilson explained as they went through the huge doorway.

Inside the exhibit the lights were dim. A few members of the museum's facilities team were there working. They tightened screws, installed signs and markers, and placed the last of the models in their places.

The kids followed the path through the exhibit as it curved and weaved around the displays. The floor beneath their feet was designed to look like a rocky path cutting through an ice- and snow-covered plain. The walls showed startlingly realistic images of a wintry landscape.

Everything looked cold, dry, and a little magical.

But what really caught the kids' attention were the realistic, animated models of huge animals: mastodons, saber-tooth cats, giant sloths, giant armadillos, dire wolves, and . . .

"Humans?" Clementine said.

She hurried along the path and stopped in front of a group of what looked like human beings. They wore clothes made of animal skins and furs. One man carried short spears. Another carried a bundle of dead rabbits tied in a sling over his shoulder. The scenery behind the group showed a herd of woolly mammoths plodding across the frozen landscape.

"Want to see them in action?" a member of the facilities team asked as he passed by.

When the kids nodded, the worker leaned toward the back of the display and plugged something in. Immediately the automated models started to turn their heads and raise their arms. Some even laughed, as if they enjoyed being with each other. The baby in a woman's arms fussed and pushed against her mother.

"They look so real," Amal said, leaning close to the Ice Age mother. The model's face was decorated with blue and silver paint. Her baby's nose was covered in white paint, and each eyebrow bore clumps of red.

"But wait a second," Clementine said. She turned and crossed her arms as she glared at Wilson. "I thought you said this was an exhibit on prehistoric mammals."

"Right . . . ," Wilson said slowly, confused as to where Clem was going with her train of thought.

"Then why are *they* here?"
Clementine asked. She pointed at
the painted humans as if they were
criminals caught in the act.

"Oh," Wilson said. "I see. You
didn't know that humans and woolly
mammoths lived at the same time."

"They did not!" Clementine said,
rolling her eyes. "Next you'll tell me
that T. rex hunted my great-grandpa!"

Amal laughed. Raining shook his
head.

"It's true," Wilson said. "I mean,
the woolly mammoth part. Not the
T. rex hunting your great-grandpa.
Some paleontologists believe
hominids—early humans—may
have contributed to the extinction of

lots of these animals, including woolly mammoths."

Clementine shook her head. "Wow," she said. "Humans have been causing trouble for wildlife since they first showed up, huh?"

They walked through the rest of the new exhibit in silence.

"I can't wait to see it with all the models in action," Raining said as they exited. "It's really cool."

"Agreed," Wilson said. "But I don't know if it compares to this . . ." He led them across the hall and into the dinosaur exhibit.

"Oh no. Not again," Amal said. "Wilson, seriously. I don't think I can handle another walk through the dinos."

The dinosaur exhibit was Wilson's favorite place in the world. His friends had been through it more times than all the fingers on all their hands combined.

"Aw, come on," Wilson said. "Mom worked with the display artists to improve the lighting and sound effects in the Jurassic section and I . . ." He stopped short in front of a display of feathered, colorful raptors. "Is this a joke?"

"What's wrong?" Clementine asked, stepping up next to him. "Are these, um, giant chickens the wrong shade of green?"

"Giant ch—" Wilson began. He shook his head to chase away the bizarre question and pointed to the back of the display. "No, Clem, nothing is wrong with the *raptors*. But everything is wrong with *that*."

The motorized raptors bent and flapped their useless proto-wings as they scurried across the display. Behind them, in clothes similar to the ones seen in the Ice Age exhibit, stood a lean and painted figure—a human. He carried a spear and seemed to be stalking the feathered dinosaurs.

"So what's the problem?" Clem asked.

"The problem," Wilson said, shaking his head, "is that when Deinonychus

hunted their prey there were definitely no humans hunting *them*."

"How do you know?" Raining Sam asked.

"Because," Wilson said, "there *were* no humans at all!"

## CHAPTER 2
## Theories

"I don't get it," Clementine said as she, Amal, and Raining walked quickly behind Wilson through the halls of the museum. "If there were people hunting woolly mammoths and saber-tooth tigers—"

"Saber-tooth cats," Wilsons corrected her. "No such thing as saber-tooth tigers."

Clementine ignored him and went on: "—then there were probably people hunting dinosaurs," she joked, "especially ones that looked like chickens."

"Imagine how many chicken nuggets they could have made from one of those!" Raining said, cracking himself up.

"Be serious, Clementine," Amal said, giving her friend a look. "Woolly mammoths didn't appear for millions and millions of years after the dinosaurs vanished."

"Not to mention humans," Wilson said. "When dinosaurs ruled Earth, mankind's closest cousin living was a big shrew."

"Ah," Clementine said, nodding as if she understood now. "Evolution."

"What about it?" Wilson asked.

"Well, it's a theory, right?" Clementine said, shrugging. "That means it might be true, but it might not be."

"Not exactly," Wilson said, getting a little frustrated. Clementine was his closest friend in the world, but sometimes her artsy nature didn't match up with his scientific way of thinking. But he was walking too quickly—and too out of breath—to argue more.

Clementine's height and long legs helped her keep pace with Wilson as he hurried toward his mother's office, located toward the rear of the museum. He had to report the misplaced hominid.

Together the group zipped past the rear entryway where they'd come in earlier. A group of girls stood near the doors. Among them was Ruthie Rothchild.

Clementine gasped. She and Ruthie weren't exactly the best of friends, to say the least. Ruthie spent a lot of time hanging around the museums too, and she always seemed to go out of her way to be mean to Clementine.

"Oh, hello, Tangerine Sim," Ruthie said. The other girls giggled. "I *love* the shade of yellow paint on your shirt this morning."

Clementine clenched her teeth. She was always painting or sculpting or drawing. That meant she often had the remnants of art supplies somewhere on her skin or clothes. But she refused to let Ruthie get the best of her. She didn't even look at Ruthie as the four friends hurried by.

"Forget about her," Amal said once they were past.

"Wilson," Clementine said, as she swallowed back her anger at Ruthie. "This is exactly what I meant about 'theories.' Remember a couple of weeks ago? *You* had a theory about the new janitor being the one responsible for the vandalism in the second-floor bathroom."

"But it wasn't her," Raining said. "It was that new guy on the security team."

"So Wilson's theory was wrong," Clementine said.

"Right, but that's different," Wilson argued.

"I don't see how," Clementine replied.

The four friends came to the door marked MUSEUM STAFF ONLY. It didn't even slow them down. Wilson pushed it open, and they all went through.

"Because that theory wasn't scientific," Amal said. "A scientific theory is an explanation for something in the natural world. It's backed up by facts and observed in repeated experiments."

It was no surprise that Amal was on Wilson's side. She and Wilson loved two very different fields of science, but they were both scientists at heart.

"Theories are accepted by scientists as true," Wilson said. "The type of theory I had about Ruthie? If it had been about science it would be called a hypothesis."

"So evolution is . . . definitely true?" Clementine said. "Like, one-hundred percent?"

"Pretty much!" Wilson said.

They stopped in front of Dr. Kipper's office.

"Here's Mom's office," Wilson said,
one hand on the doorknob. "She'll want
to know about the vandalism."

"Wait a second," Raining said, grabbing Wilson by the wrist. "Vandalism?"

"Yeah," Clementine said. "I didn't know we were reporting a crime! I figured it was just a mistake."

"Who would make that mistake?" Wilson said, bewildered.

"Anyone could have made a mistake, Wilson," Raining said. "It's human nature. Someone on the facilities team could have gotten confused and accidentally put the human in the dino display. That's not that unbelievable."

Wilson frowned. "Maybe," he admitted. "But either way, we should tell my mom. It has to be fixed.

The museum has been open for fifteen minutes already. Just think of how many people have already seen the display!"

The door flung open. Wilson's mother, Dr. Carolyn Kipper, stood on the other side.

"Oh!" Dr. Kipper said, looking surprised. "Wilson. I thought I heard voices out here. What have you kids been up to?"

"There's a problem in the dino exhibit, Mom," Wilson said. Briefly he recapped the misplaced hominid they'd seen.

"I'm sure it's just an error, Dr. Kipper," Raining said.

"Error or not," Dr. Kipper said, "it needs to be corrected. I'll get facilities down there at once. Thanks, kids."

With that, she closed the office door.

## CHAPTER 3
## The Painted Hunter

The four friends headed back to the main gallery. They didn't hurry now, since Wilson's mom was undoubtedly on top of the problem.

"I wonder how that could have happened," Wilson said, still thinking about the incorrect exhibit.

"It was probably just a mistake," Clementine said, "like Raining said."

"Yeah," Raining said. "After all, Clementine and I know next to nothing about when humans first evolved, or when dinosaurs went extinct, or why there were giant green chickens, or—"

"OK, OK," Wilson said. "So I've failed completely in giving my best friends even a basic understanding of my favorite branch of science."

"Aw," Clementine said. She put an arm around her younger friend. "Don't feel bad. Ask Amal how much I know about space and stuff."

"She thinks the Andromeda galaxy is the newest mobile phone," Amal said.

"It isn't?" Clementine said with a wink.

Wilson rolled his eyes and laughed. "You guys could be right. But it's hard to believe anyone on staff here at the museum could make a mistake like that," he said.

Just then he spotted a pair of people farther down the hallway. "Hey, look. There are Phil and Maureen from facilities."

He led his friends at a faster pace to catch up with Phil and Maureen in the dinosaur hall. The two strong members of the facilities team carried the painted hominid hunter between them.

"Hey, Wilson," Maureen said when she caught sight of the group of kids. She sounded annoyed and tired.

"Can you believe this?" Phil said, sounding just as irritated as his partner. "I could have sworn Mo and I just moved this guy last night."

"Into the dinosaur exhibit?" Wilson asked.

Maureen shook her head. "Of course not. We put him with his friends across the hall," she said.

"And this guy isn't exactly a lightweight, ya know?" Phil said, grunting.

"Well, how'd he get into the dinosaur exhibit then?" Clementine asked. "You two didn't move him?"

"It wasn't us," Maureen said, shaking her head again.

"Must have been one of the braniacs with an office," Phil said. He glanced at Wilson. "No offense to your mother, of course. I'm sure it wasn't her."

"None taken," Wilson said. "I know it wasn't her."

"But it's a little weird, don't you think?" Maureen said. "Even we know humans don't belong in the dino hall. I doubt any of the doctors would make that mistake."

Wilson and his friends watched as Phil and Maureen carried the hunter into the Ice Age exhibit. Both workers' arms strained against the sleeves of their facilities uniform. The painted hunter was obviously very heavy.

*Too heavy to have moved on his own,* Wilson thought. *So how did he end up in the wrong hall?*

## CHAPTER 4
## Dr. Snapper

A few minutes later, the four friends sat together at a small table near the window in the cafeteria. They each had a hot chocolate.

"OK," Raining said. "I admit it—it doesn't sound like that hominid being in the wrong exhibit was an error. Someone definitely moved it there on purpose."

"Agreed," Clementine said. "It doesn't sound like anyone on staff would think a human hunter belonged in there."

Wilson, sitting next to Clementine and across from Raining, nodded. "Now we need to figure out *why* someone would do this," he said. "We have a mystery to solve."

Beside him, Clementine suddenly tensed.

"What is it?" Wilson asked.

"Ruthie," Clementine said, nodding toward the line of people at the cashier station. "And she's staring at me."

Wilson, Amal, and Raining all glanced in the direction she'd nodded. Sure enough, Ruthie was standing in

line waiting to pay for her food. An
older woman, about the same age as
Dr. Kipper and wearing a museum staff
badge, stood with her.

"Ignore her, Clem," Raining said. "She's trying to upset you."

"Yeah," Amal said. "It's her favorite pastime." She shot a glare at the bully girl.

"Who's she's with?" Wilson asked, turning back around.

"I think we're about to find out," Raining said. "They're headed this way."

"Clementine Wim, is that you?" the woman asked, approaching their table.

"Um, yes," Clementine said, looking surprised.

"I thought I recognized you. I'm Dr. Snapper, Ruthie's mom," the woman continued. "You've been in Ruthie's classes for years. I remember you in preschool, with your wild red hair and that big smile of yours. Look how you've grown up!"

"Oh, yeah," Clementine said, blushing a bit. "I guess Ruthie and I were friends back then." They had been, back when they were very little. Clementine couldn't remember quite when Ruthie got mean. But she sure had and fast.

As if to prove Clementine right, Ruthie glared at her just then.

"What are you doing at the museum?" Clementine asked.

"I'm the new professor of anthropology," Dr. Snapper said. "I specialize in paleoanthropology."

"Pally-what?" Amal said.

"Paleoanthropology," Dr. Snapper said. "I study early hominids and how they might have lived, what their cultures might have been like, that sort of thing."

"My mom told me there was a new professor starting," Wilson said. "I didn't realize you were Ruthie's mom. She said you're a leader in your field."

"Well I don't know about that," Dr. Snapper said, blushing. "But I'm certainly happy to be here. We'll let you kids eat. Nice to see you." With that, Dr. Snapper led Ruthie to a nearby table.

"Wow," Clementine said once Ruthie and her mom had left. "Her job actually sounds pretty interesting.

I can't believe a woman with such a brilliant mind would raise such a terrible daughter."

"We might not have a motive yet," Amal said, leaning back in her chair and crossing her arms, "but now that we know her mom is on staff here, we clearly have a prime suspect: Ruthie."

## CHAPTER 5
## Heavy Objects

Raining shook his head as the four friends discussed the case. "I just don't think it could have been Ruthie," he said.

"Why not?" Clementine asked, throwing out her empty hot chocolate cup. "She's the absolute worst. She'd probably do something like that just for laughs."

Clementine narrowed her eyes, getting worked up as she thought about all the stunts Ruthie had pulled over the years.

There was the time she'd *accidentally* put a bowl of spaghetti and meat sauce on Clementine's cafeteria chair at the Capitol City Art Museum just before she sat down.

Or the time in third grade when Ruthie had discovered Clementine reading quietly under the willow tree at recess. Long story short, Clementine had smelled like rotten eggs for three days.

And of course there was the time at the Air and Space Museum, when Ruthie had somehow managed to replace the planetarium show with a video of Clementine—complete with paint all over her face.

"She loves chaos," Clementine continued, getting worked up. "She harnesses bad energy and soaks it up like a plant soaks up sunlight. She drinks tears."

"That's all true," Raining said, trying not to laugh. "But even Ruthie couldn't move one of those human models. Remember how hard Phil and Maureen had to work to carry the painted hunter?"

Wilson nodded. "It weighed a lot," he agreed. "Ruthie may be evil, but she's no supervillain. No way she could lift one of those."

"Not on her own. But what if she had help? Her  mom's help?" Clementine said.

"I doubt it," Amal said, shaking her head. "Even if her mom is responsible for creating Ruthie, why would she be willing to hurt the museum? She just got a job here."

Clementine was silent a moment, still glaring at Ruthie and Dr. Snapper. "I'll be right back," she said. She stood up and walked over to Ruthie and her mom.

"Um, can we *help* you?" Ruthie said, sounding disgusted.

"I hope so," Clementine said. Her voice shook a bit.

"What the heck is she doing?" Amal whispered to Raining and Wilson.

Both boys shrugged.

Clementine put one hand on a huge plastic crate that sat against the wall. It was marked GARRISON DAIRY.

"Can you two help me move this?" she asked the mother and daughter. She raised her voice so her friends could make out what she'd said.

"That sounds like a job for the people who work in the cafeteria," Dr. Snapper said, looking confused.

"Yeah," Ruthie said, sneering. "Why do you want to move that anyway?"

"Um, just trying to help out Phil and Maureen," Clementine said, thinking quickly. "I told them I'd move this into the kitchen."

"So use a dolly," Ruthie said. She stood up. "Come on, Mom. I think your break is over." With that, Ruthie and her mom rose from their table and left.

"Well," Clementine said, walking back to her own table and dropping into her seat next to Wilson, "that didn't work at all."

"It was a nice try, Clementine," Raining said.

Just then a big man wearing a white shirt and tan pants—the cafeteria uniform—came out of the kitchen. "Hi, Wilson," he said.

"Hi, Alvin," Wilson replied.

As the four friends watched, Alvin stepped up to the big crate of milk. Like it was nothing, he wrapped his arms around the crate, lifted it up from the floor, and carried it into the kitchen.

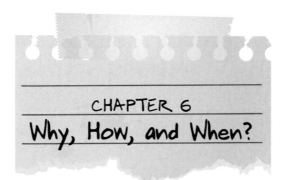

## CHAPTER 6
## Why, How, and When?

"I think we're looking at this the wrong way," Amal said. "First, we need a motive. Why would someone *want* to move that painted hunter into the dino hall?"

"To cause trouble," Clementine said. "You know that's good enough for Ruthie, and the acorn doesn't fall far from the tree. It's probably enough for Dr. Snapper too."

"That's not much of a motive," Amal pointed out.

"Especially for the newest member of the museum's staff," Wilson agreed. "Dr. Snapper would lose her job if they got caught. It wouldn't be worth the risk."

"Besides," Raining said, "motive isn't the only issue."

"Right," Wilson said. "There's motive, means, and opportunity."

"Pretty much why, how, and when," Amal added.

"That big guy in the cafeteria has the means," Raining said. "Did you see how easily he picked up that huge shipment of milk?"

Wilson nodded. "He probably had opportunity too," he said. "The cafeteria staff starts way before opening. I always smell coffee brewing and cinnamon rolls baking when Mom and I come in. That means the food staff is obviously already here and working."

"But he has no motive," Raining pointed out. "Why would he care about moving that figure?"

"Besides, Alvin is the nicest guy in the world," Wilson added. "He'd never do anything if he wasn't a hundred-percent certain he was supposed to."

Amal elbowed Clementine gently. "Maybe it's a member of the public who happens to think humans did hunt giant chickens and that evolution is just a theory," she said with a laugh. "That's a motive."

Clementine's face turned red. "Oh, shush," she said.

## CHAPTER 7
## Time Travel

The next morning, the protestors in front of the museum were at it again.

"I wish they'd leave us alone," Dr. Kipper said as she and Wilson weaved between the group of protestors and made their way into the museum.

"Don't they have the right to protest?" Wilson asked.

"Of course they do," Dr. Kipper said. "But their ideas are so . . . backward. A flat Earth that's not even seven thousand years old? This stuff has been disproven over and over again by real science."

"Does it make it you feel like you're wasting your time with your work?" Wilson asked. "If people just believe stuff like that?"

"In a way," Dr. Kipper said. "I'm just glad there are kids like *you* and your friends, who really care about and understand science."

They went into the staff-only back hallway. Almost immediately they bumped into Dr. Snapper.

"Oh, good morning, Dr. Snapper," said Dr. Kipper. "Everything going OK so far?"

Dr. Snapper sighed. "I'm afraid not," she said. "I'm on my way to the dinosaur exhibit right now. It seems another early human model has found its way five million years into the past."

Wilson's eyebrows shot up at that. "Mom, I'm going to meet my friends out front," he said quickly. He hurried off, hoping to beat Dr. Snapper to the scene of the crime.

Just outside the dinosaur hall, Wilson spotted his three best friends, right where they'd agreed to meet.

"Oh no," Amal said when she saw the panicked look on Wilson's face. "Again?"

Wilson nodded. "Come on," he said. "Maybe there will be a clue this time."

The four young sleuths dashed into the dinosaur hall. This time the misplaced human was a woman in simple, colorful clothes. Her face was painted white, except just above her eyes, where it was rich red. She stood among a trio of baby triceratops.

"She's scary," Amal said.

"I think she's beautiful," Clementine said. "I want to paint her."

"Excuse me, kids," Dr. Snapper said as she hurried up to the display. She stepped carefully over the guardrail, making sure not to snag her suit on the triceratops' horns, and wrapped her arms around the woman with the painted face.

Dr. Snapper heaved. She strained. She huffed and puffed and sweated and groaned. But she couldn't move the hominid. Finally she gave up and wiped her brow. "Well, I hoped to spare the good people in facilities a trip, but I don't think I can lift this woman on my own," she said.

"How'd she get here, anyway?" Clementine asked. She wasn't sure it was safe to chat with Ruthie's mom, but she decided to risk it.

"I'm afraid I have no idea how this Ice Age woman got here from the exhibit across the hall," Dr. Snapper said. "All I know is that she's too heavy to move easily, and she didn't walk on her own."

"I don't see what the big deal is," said a voice nearby.

The four friends and Dr. Snapper
turned. On a bench against the nearby
wall sat a woman. She wore a white
shirt, tan pants, and a baseball cap
pulled low over her face. She took a sip
from a cardboard coffee cup.

"After all," the woman went on as she lowered her coffee, "all this stuff is just theories, right? No one knows what *really* happened. Lots of people think the world is only a few thousand years old."

She stood up and took one last sip of her coffee.

"Actually," Dr. Snapper said, "a *scientific* theory isn't like a theory the way you would use the word in normal conversation. In fact—"

But before Dr. Snapper could explain further, the woman tossed her empty cup into a trash can and walked away.

## CHAPTER 8

# Ruthie's Righteous Rage

Wilson paced back and forth in front of the Ice Age exhibit. His three friends sat on a bench behind him. Clementine leaned forward, deep in thought. Raining drummed his fingers on his forehead. Amal tapped one foot impatiently.

"Dr. Snapper is obviously innocent," Wilson said as he paced. "We saw her struggle to lift that model."

"Or she was faking it," Amal said, "to throw us off her trail."

"Or she had help when she moved them," Raining said.

"Like Ruthie, for example," Clementine offered.

Wilson shook his head. "I admit she had the means," he said, "and the opportunity, since she works here. But I can't buy the motive. Her work is all about early human culture. She'd want the displays to be correct."

"I guess," Clementine said. "And she was nice to me, even if Ruthie can't be bothered to do the same."

"Maybe we shouldn't rule out Ruthie, then," Amal suggested.

"You think *she* could lift one of those human models alone?" Raining said.

"Well . . . no," Amal said.

"She did suggest using a dolly to move the crate of milk when I asked for help," Clementine pointed out. "Maybe she has some experience with using a dolly around here—like to move a hominid model!"

Wilson wasn't convinced, but he shrugged. "I suppose we should question her," he said.

Clementine stood up. "Is she here today?" she asked.

Wilson shook his head. "I haven't seen her," he said. "But it's a big place."

"Well, then I guess we'd better start looking," Raining said with a sigh. The four friends headed out of the Ice Age hall—and immediately bumped into a crowd of museum visitors. Several wore shirts with slogans like THE EARTH IS YOUNG and WE ARE NOT MONKEYS. The crowd pushed past them and into the Ice Age exhibit.

"What are they doing in here?" Amal said. "Those antiscience types won't get anything out of this exhibit."

"Maybe they're hoping to make sure no one else does either," Wilson said. "Look."

The friends glanced back into the Ice Age hall. It was nearly full now—full of antiscience protestors.

A guard stood in the doorway to make sure no one else entered the exhibit until the crowd thinned. That was the law—the fire marshal determined how many people could safely be in a room of the museum, and the museum had to be sure that crowds never got bigger than that.

"They're making it awfully hard for guests who are actually interested in giant mammals to get in to have a look," Clementine said. "That's so inconsiderate."

"For once you and I agree about something," said Ruthie as she appeared next to Clementine. The mean girl glared at the crowd of protestors. "That's my mom's pet project. She's been

working on it day and night for weeks. Now these jokers are ruining it."

Clementine gave her a surprised look. "So, you don't agree with them?"

Ruthie laughed scornfully. "Are you kidding. Flat Earth?" she said as she crossed her arms. "Haven't these people ever seen a photo of Earth from space? Or been on an airplane? Or to the beach—or anywhere else with a horizon?"

Amal nodded. "We have loads of pictures right next door at the Air and Space Museum. And it's free to enter. They can all have a look."

"And antievolution?" Ruthie said. "Um, please. My mother has spent the past fifteen years studying hominid evolution. Do they think she was just doing it for fun?"

"I might be crazy," Clementine said to Ruthie, "but are you on our side this time?"

"I just want my mom's new project to go well," Ruthie said. For once her voice sounded kind and sincere.

"Then it wasn't you who moved the early human into the dino hall?" Clementine blurted out.

Ruthie's mouth fell open. "Me?" she said. "Why would I do that?"

"You *do* like to cause trouble," Clementine said.

Ruthie laughed. "Yeah, for you guys," she snapped. "Not for my mom."

With that she walked off, shaking her head. "Dork," Ruthie muttered as she disappeared around the corner.

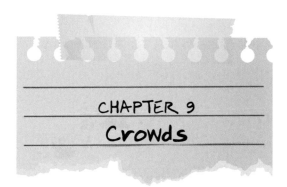

## CHAPTER 9
## Crowds

"So where does that leave us?" Wilson asked a few minutes later. "It wasn't Ruthie. And it wasn't her mom."

"What about Phil and Maureen?" Amal suggested. "We know they have the means. They're both as strong as linebackers."

Wilson shook his head. "I don't think so," he said. "You heard how annoyed they were at having to move that painted hunter back to his proper place."

A line had formed outside the Ice Age hall now, with people eager to get in. But no one could enter until the protestors made room for them.

"What about the protestors?" Wilson said. "They have a motive: They're antiscience, and they're against anything that contradicts their belief that Earth is only a few thousand years old."

"Putting a human model in the dino hall would definitely fit into their world view," Amal added.

"Yeah," Clementine said, "but what about opportunity and means? When could they have done it? And how?"

"There are at least a hundred protestors," Raining said. "Picking up the models definitely wouldn't be a problem."

"But when?" Wilson said. "Both times, the vandal struck when the museum was closed. First on Sunday evening—after close—or Monday morning before opening. Same thing this time—it had to have been moved early this morning or late last night."

"Hasn't the museum been open for a while?" Amal asked. "They could have done it the moment the doors opened."

Wilson shook his head again. "The museum opens at ten on Tuesdays," he said. He sat on a bench and held his head in his hands. "I know we're missing something."

"But what?" Raining said. "We're out of suspects."

Wilson tried to focus, but the noise of the crowd made it hard. "Ugh!" he exclaimed. "It's so crowded, I can hardly think. Some days they trickle in, and some days they just fill the place the second the museum opens."

Suddenly he gasped. "The museum opens at ten!" he said.

"So?" Amal asked. "You already said that."

"It's ten a.m. right now," Wilson pointed out. "Well, technically it's five after. But we were all in the dino hall with Dr. Snapper about a half hour ago, right?"

His three friends shrugged.

"So?" Amal asked again. "We already established that the crimes happened during museum off hours."

"*So*," Wilson said, "that means that anyone here before ten this morning must have been museum staff—or one of their kids."

"Like us and Ruthie," Clementine said.

"Yup," Wilson said. "So who else was there when we checked the scene of the crime earlier this morning? Think about it."

"Just us," Raining said after a moment. "And Dr. Snapper, of course."

Wilson looked from one friend to the other. "But wasn't there someone else?" he asked.

"Oh yeah," Amal drawled. "That rude lady with the coffee."

"She was in the museum long before the doors opened to the public," Clementine concluded, "and that means she works here."

"Or her parent works here," Raining said.

His three friends looked at him like he was crazy.

"I mean, it's *possible*," he said. "But, yeah. Probably that first thing."

## CHAPTER 10
## Alibi for Alvin

The four young sleuths stood together in the hallway outside the Ice Age hall.

"So how come we haven't seen this lady around the museum before?" Clementine said. She leaned on the wall next to a sign. It read CAFETERIA and had an arrow pointing down the nearby staircase.

Wilson shook his head, stumped. "I don't know," he said. "I mean, we're here a lot, but we don't know everyone. She's obviously not in my mom's department."

"Right," Amal said. "Based on what she said earlier about evolution and the age of our planet, she's clearly not super into science. That much was clear."

"So how does a person like that," Clementine said, "get a job working at a science museum?"

"It's not that strange, really," Wilson said. "A couple of weeks ago I was chatting with Alvin in the cafeteria about the T. rex skeleton in the dino hall. He suggested we add a human skeleton that looks like it's running away."

His friends laughed.

"Yeah, I laughed at first too," Wilson said. "I thought he was joking. But he wasn't kidding. I had to set him straight."

Suddenly Wilson stood up straight. "Tan pants and a white shirt!" he said, snapping his fingers. "That's what she was wearing. That's the cafeteria uniform."

"And since we didn't recognize her, she must work someplace she doesn't get a lot of face time with museum guests. Like in the kitchen," Raining said.

"With Alvin," Amal finished.

Wilson nodded. "The strongest person who works here," he said, "And probably the only one who could move one of those models alone. Come on. Let's get my mom and head to the caf."

* * *

Wilson led his friends, Dr. Kipper, and Dr. Snapper into the cafeteria. Alvin was stocking the refrigerated case with juice and soda.

"Oh, hi, Wilson," Alvin said, rising from his knees. "Dr. Kipper."

At full height, he towered over the two staff scientists, and positively

dwarfed the children. Standing next to Wilson, he looked like a giant out of a fairy tale.

"Alvin, can I ask you something?" Wilson said.

"Sure," Alvin said. "Any time. You know that. But I'm surprised a supersmart kid like you needs any help from me."

Wilson smiled. "Who's in charge here in the cafeteria?" he asked.

"Mr. Patterson," Alvin said. "You know that. He's facilities director, and the cafeteria is officially part of facilities."

"Right," Wilson said, "but who's in charge of day-to-day operations? Not Mr. Patterson, right?"

"Oh, you mean the cafeteria manager?" Alvin said. "That would

Javier—Javier Sills. Do you need to see him?"

Wilson shook his head and sighed, disappointed. "I thought for sure it would be the woman we met earlier," he said

"Is there another manager?" Amal tried. "Like, an assistant to Mr. Sills or something?"

"Oh, sure," Alvin said, nodding. "Javier doesn't work weekends, and Tuesday mornings he's always in meetings with Mr. Patterson, so Thelma is in charge. She's the assistant manager."

"Aha!" Clementine said.

Alvin gawked at her, surprised.

"So on Tuesday mornings and weekends," Wilson concluded, "Thelma tells you what to do, most of the time?"

"Yep," Alvin said. "She's in the kitchen right now, in fact."

"Thanks, Alvin," Wilson said. He turned to his mom and friends. "I think we should go talk to her."

"Just a second, Wilson," Alvin said.

He hurried past the four friends and the professors and blocked the doorway to the kitchen.

"One of the things Thelma asked me to do this morning was to make sure no one bugged her while she was in the back," he continued.

"Bug her? What do you mean?" Wilson asked.

The big cafeteria worker puffed out his chest and crossed his arms. "I mean, I can't let you back there. Sorry."

## CHAPTER 11
## Kitchen Crook

Wilson had known Alvin for a couple of years, but he'd never seen him looking quite so big and scary. They always got along great.

"Alvin," said Dr. Kipper, "you're obviously a loyal employee, but I'm sure if Thelma knew Dr. Snapper and I wanted to speak to her, she'd ask you to let us by."

Alvin looked at her sideways, thinking it over, and then shook his head. "Sorry, Dr. Kipper," he said. "I just can't risk it. It would go against Thelma's direct orders. I report to her. And I need this job—I can't afford to get in trouble."

Wilson led his friends a few feet away and into a huddle. Dr. Kipper and Dr. Snapper stayed with Alvin, still trying to talk their way past.

"We're on the right track," Wilson said, "but I'm not going to try to force my way past Alvin. I don't want to get him in trouble."

"What if he didn't *let* us past?" Clementine said. "What if we just happened to *get* past when he wasn't looking?"

"How would we do that?" Wilson asked.

"I'll cause a distraction," Clementine said. "You guys can rush past when he's not watching."

"What kind of distraction?" Wilson asked, sounding very unsure.

Clementine looked around. "I know!" she said. "I'll go get an ice cream cone and pretend the soft-serve machine is stuck. There'll be ice cream everywhere. It'll be great!"

"Um, let's leave that as a last resort," Wilson said. "Any other ideas?"

"You said before that Alvin hates to break the rules, right?" Amal said.

"Yeah," Wilson said.

"So," Amal said, "let's just tell him the truth. I bet he'll help us."

"You might be right," Wilson said. "Let's do it."

The four friends walked back to Alvin, where he was very stubbornly refusing to move aside for the two professors.

"Alvin," Wilson said, "I have some bad news for you."

The big man looked at Wilson with a crooked glare. "What do you mean?" he asked.

"You're my friend," Wilson said, "so I'm going to tell you the truth. Not everything Thelma has asked you to do has been on the up and up. Like moving those fake people from the Ice Age to the dino hall, for example."

Alvin's eyes went wide.

"She did ask you to do that, right?" Amal asked.

Alvin nodded slowly. "She said that new discoveries proved that dinosaurs and people lived at the same time," he said. He looked pleadingly at Wilson. "I told her that's not what you said, but she insisted."

"But you know it's not your place to alter the exhibits," Dr. Kipper said.

"That's what I told her," Alvin replied quickly. "But Thelma said that technically speaking we *are* members of the facilities staff. *And* that was on

Sunday evening after closing, when we were cleaning up the kitchen. So she was in charge."

"And this morning, before opening," Wilson added. "She was also in charge."

Alvin nodded.

Dr. Snapper put a hand on Alvin's arm. "No one's angry with you," she said, "but Thelma knew what she was doing was against the rules. We need to speak to her."

With that, Alvin finally stepped aside.

"Thanks, Alvin," Wilson said. He led his friends, his mom, and Dr. Snapper into the kitchen.

"No one's allowed back here," Thelma said when she heard them enter. She sat in a metal office chair at the manager's desk. Wilson recognized her at once as the woman who had been rude that morning in the dino hall.

When she caught sight of the group, Thelma sighed in irritation. "Alvin had one job," she said.

"Oh, knock it off," Clementine said. "Alvin deserves a better boss than you."

"Well, he'll have one soon," Dr. Kipper said as she pulled out her cell phone. "Because Thelma won't be working here much longer."

"Because Thelma is responsible for vandalizing the exhibits," Wilson concluded. "She had the means, the motive, and the opportunity."

"She works here at just the right hours to pull it off," Amal said.

"And she believes Earth is flat and young," Clementine said.

"And she has Alvin to do the heavy lifting," Raining finished.

"I guess you figured it all out," Thelma said, rising from her chair and smiling smugly. "I don't mind. I stand by my actions. Until every lie this museum puts on display is untwisted and untangled, my fellow protestors and I will continue the fight!"

"Good, then continue the fight somewhere else," Dr. Snapper said. "Because we have Mr. Patterson on the phone right now."

Dr. Kipper held up the phone with the speaker turned on. They all heard Mr. Patterson's gruff voice shout, "You're fired, Thelma! Clean out your locker and scram."

Thelma scowled at them, but just for a moment. Then she smiled, serene as you please. She picked up her purse and hat, and she left.

## CHAPTER 12
## The New Girl

It was the next morning, and the four friends lay on the grass of the Big Lawn behind their four museums.

"Where is she?" Amal said.

"She should be here any minute," Wilson said. "This is where I said we'd meet her."

"I can't believe she asked to join us," Raining said.

"Ugh," Clementine said. "My stomach hurts just thinking about it."

"So think about something else," Amal suggested.

They were quiet a moment. Finally Clementine spoke. "I hope Alvin won't get in any trouble," she said. "He's really a nice guy."

"Nah," Wilson said. "I talked to my mom, and everyone in administration and facilities knows he was only doing what Thelma told him to do. He got a warning, that's all."

Just then, Wilson sat up and looked toward the museum. "Here she comes," he said.

Clementine sat up beside him. "I'm so not ready for this," she said.

"You'll be fine," Amal said, taking her hand.

"Yeah," Raining said. He put an arm around Clementine's shoulders. "We're right here with you."

Clementine gritted her teeth and nodded.

They sat together and watched the small figure walk up the slope toward them. She stopped on the flat rock and stood there, looking down at them.

"Look, dorks," Ruthie said. "Sorry to burst your bubble, but I won't be joining your weird museum friends . . . *thing*."

"You won't?" Wilson said. "But when we texted yesterday you said you wanted to and—"

"Yeah, well," Ruthie interrupted, "forget all that. My mom just got an offer for *much* better job chairing the anthropology department at Capitol University, so . . . bye, or whatever."

With that, she sneered, turned, and walked back down the slope.

Clementine sighed. "I don't know if I'm relieved or disappointed," she said.

Wilson shook his head slowly. "Relieved," he said. "Definitely relieved."

Steve B.

## About the Author

Steve Brezenoff is the author of more than fifty middle-grade chapter books, including the Field Trip Mysteries series, the Ravens Pass series of thrillers, and the Return to Titanic series. In his spare time, he enjoys video games, cycling, and cooking. Steve lives in Minneapolis with his wife, Beth, and their son and daughter.

Lisa W.

## About the Illustrator

Lisa K. Weber is an illustrator currently living in Oakland, California. She graduated from Parsons School of Design in 2000 and then began freelancing. Since then, she has completed many print, animation, and design projects, including graphic novelizations of classic literature, character and background designs for children's cartoons, and textiles for dog clothing.

# Glossary

**automated** (aw-TAH-may-tehd)—a mechanical process that is programmed to follow a set of instructions

**controversial** (kon-truh-VUR-shuhl)—causing dispute or disagreement

**facilities** (fuh-SIL-uh-tees)—a department of people responsible for the operations of the building or company

**hypothesis** (hye-POTH-uh-siss)—a prediction that can be tested about how a scientific investigation or experiment will turn out

**motive** (MOH-tiv)—reason why someone does something

**protestors** (pro-TEST-ohrs)—people who object to something strongly and publicly

**remnans** (REM-nuhnts)—pieces or parts of something that are left over

**vandalism** (VAN-duhl-ihzm)—intentional destruction or defacement of property

# DISCUSSION QUESTIONS

**1.** Wilson has a more scientific mind, while Clementine has a more artistic one. Who do you think you are more like and why?

**2.** It's important that the museum displays are accurate, even if some people don't agree with them. What are some reasons given in the story for this?

**3.** The sleuths see Ruthie as a suspect, but in the end, she actually helps out with their case. Do you think she could ever actually be friends with the group?

# WRITING PROMPTS

**1.** The protestors outside the museum argue against scientific facts, which upsets Dr. Kipper. Write a letter from Wilson's perspective telling Dr. Kipper why her work is important.

**2.** The Natural History Museum has a lot of interesting exhibits. Which one would you be most interested in seeing? Pick one from this book and write a paragraph explaining your choice.

**3.** Alvin felt he had to do what Thelma told him or he'd lose his job. Imagine you were in Alvin's shoes. What would you have done? Write a few paragraphs detailing how you would have handled the situation.

# MORE ABOUT HOMINIDS

Have you ever wondered how human beings evolved? How we went from apes to the walking, talking, critical-thinking creatures we are today? We have hominids to thank—at least in part. Hominids were an early family of humans, the ancient ancestors of modern human beings.

The earliest hominid scientists have discovered is called *Sahelanthropus tchadensis*. The bones of this particular hominid are roughly 6–7 million years old. There is some debate about whether or not *Sahelanthropus tchadensis* is the real ancestor of modern humans or a side branch. Some scientists argue that another hominid, *Orrorin tugenensis*, is the true ancestor of modern humans. Bones of the two differed species were discovered in 2001, but so far there haven't been enough discoveries to say who the true ancestor is.

# WHO—OR WHAT— WAS LUCY?

Perhaps the most famous hominid scientists have discovered so far is "Lucy"—the first *Australopithecus afarensis* skeleton ever found.

- Lucy was discovered in 1974 by paleontologist Donald C. Johanson. He uncovered her bones in Africa—Hadar, Ethiopia to be exact.

- Lucy's bones are 3.2 million years old. Today, her remains are still only about 40% complete.

- Based on Lucy's skeleton, scientists were able to determine that she had both human and ape features and stood approximately three and a half feet tall. They were able to tell that she was a hominid because she walked upright.

- Lucy was named after the Beatles song, "Lucy in the Sky with Diamonds," which was played on repeat the day "Lucy" was first discovered.

# Ready for more MYSTERY?

# MUSEUM MYSTERIES

Check out the Capitol City sleuths'
next adventure and help them solve
crime in some of the city's
most important museums!

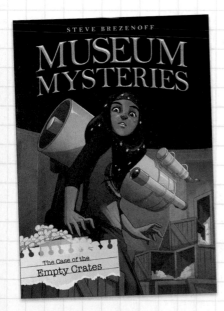

The Air and Space Museum is
adding a new exhibit, and Amal
Farah and her friends get
to attend the grand opening!
But before the new exhibit
goes live, some of the items
go missing. This won't be
good—the exhibit is funded
by a rich local businessman,
and without the objects to
show, the exhibit can't open.
Did another museum take
the object, trying to make
up for missing funding?
Was it a thief interested
in telescopes? Or someone else? Amal and her friends are
determined to solve this crazy mystery!